Do-It-Yourself Noddy

It was a sunny morning in Toy Town…

BRRING! BRRING!
A sleepy Noddy switched off his alarm clock.
"That's better," he mumbled. "But why did
I want to wake up early?"

"Of course!" Noddy cried, leaping out of bed.
"It's my kite day!"

He dashed over to the table. "And here is my
very own kite kit!" he said. "I'll have breakfast
and get dressed really quickly."

I'll build my lovely kite and add a knotted tail.
If she's put together right, into the sky she'll sail!
Noddy sang this song as he made his toast.
"Jam today, I think," he said, trying to twist
the lid off the jar.

"Oh dear!" said Noddy, as he struggled.
"I can't open this jar."

"Maybe Mr Sparks has a tool I can use?" said Noddy. He jumped into his car and drove off.

But Mr Sparks' garage was shut.

"Oh, bother!" wailed Noddy. "How am I going to get the lid off that jar?"

Then Noddy had a bright idea. "Big-Ears will know what to do!"

Noddy screeched to a halt outside his friend's house.

"Big-Ears, I need your help!" he shouted.

The front door swung open and Big-Ears rushed out.

"What's wrong, Noddy?" he asked.

Noddy held out the jar. "I can't get the lid off."

Big-Ears looked cross. "Noddy! I thought you were in real trouble."

"But it *is* an emergency," cried Noddy. "I can't have my breakfast until I open this jar!"

Big-Ears sighed as he looked at the jam jar.
"Look," he said. "It has a little ring on the
top. Just pull it gently and the lid pops off."
"Oh," said Noddy, peering at it in surprise.

"I'm sure," said Big-Ears, sternly, "you could have worked that out for yourself."

"Oh, but you're much cleverer than I am, Big-Ears," laughed Noddy. "I'd much rather you did it."

He started his car. "Thanks, Big-Ears."

When Noddy arrived home he raced upstairs to get dressed. He soon had all his clothes on. But there was a problem.

"Oh, bother, my shoelaces are undone. I hate tying bows… I know! I'll ask Big-Ears. He'll do them up in a jiffy!"

Noddy drove quickly to Big-Ears' house again.

"Big-Ears, come quick! I need your help!"
he called.

His friend opened the front door. "I was
just about to have a bath, Noddy. Is it a real
emergency this time?" Big-Ears asked.

"I can't tie my shoelaces," said Noddy, waving
one foot in the air. "Will you do them up for me?"

"Oh, Noddy. Didn't you even try to do it
yourself?" asked Big-Ears.

"Well, no," said Noddy. "It's much easier
for you to do it!"

"*Easier!*" cried Big-Ears as he tied Noddy's laces. "What rubbish! Think of the time you waste driving across town every time you need help. You're a clever boy, you can do these things for yourself."

But Noddy wasn't listening. He wanted to make his kite.

Noddy jumped back into his car.

"You're so good at solving my problems, Big-Ears," he said. "I don't know what I'd do without you."

Big-Ears shook his head. "That boy needs to think for himself." Then Big-Ears grinned.

He had a plan.

"At last, I'm ready to make my kite," said Noddy,
spreading out all the things on his table.

"Paper, sticks, string. But it's just too difficult!
I don't know where to start!"

He bundled everything into the box and ran
to the door. Big-Ears would know what to do!

PARP! PARP! PARP! PARP! Noddy beeped his horn
outside Big-Ears' house.

But this time there was no answer.

"That's odd," he murmured. "Where is Big-Ears?"
Then he spotted a note pinned to the front door.

To anyone who knocks,
I shall be gone all day.
See you this evening.
Big-Ears.

"Oh, no!" cried Noddy. "Now I can't fly my kite today. I need Big-Ears to put it together for me."

Just then, Noddy saw a funny little man walking towards Big-Ears' house.

"My name is Mr Sham," said the man. "Forgive me for bothering you, but I really need help."

Noddy looked at him. "Oh? So do I," he said.

Mr Sham held out a box. "I noticed you had a kit rather like mine," he said.

"Mine's a kite, what's yours?" Noddy asked, politely.
"Well," said Mr Sham, "I need a shelf for all my
books, so I bought myself a do-it-yourself shelf kit.
The trouble is, I have no idea how to put it together.
Can you help me?"

Noddy shook his head sadly. "Sorry, no. Big-Ears would know how to do it, but he won't be home until tonight."

"Well, let's pretend you are Big-Ears," said Mr Sham. "What would he tell us to do first?"

"Let's see…" Noddy thought. "He'd probably tell us to check all the pieces first."

"Good thinking!" cried Mr Sham and he and
Noddy tipped out all the pieces. "What next?"
"There's a picture on the lid," said Noddy.
"I think Big-Ears would look at the picture
to see where each piece goes."

Noddy stared at the picture. "Those are the things that hold the shelf up at either end."

Mr Sham tried to bang nails in with his fist. "Ouch!" he said. "How would Big-Ears stick the nails into the shelf?"

"He'd use a hammer!" cried Noddy and, piece by piece, they made the shelf.

"We've done it!" cried Noddy, proudly.

"*You* did it!" said Mr Sham. "But there's one more problem. This is brown. All my other shelves are blue."

Noddy was now getting rather good at solving problems. "Oh, that's easy!" he laughed.
"We'll paint it!"

When they had finished, they admired the shelf.

"It's beautiful! Thank you, Noddy. I could never have done it without you," said Mr Sham.

Noddy blushed. "You're welcome. But I just used Big-Ears' ideas."

Mr Sham smiled. "But, Noddy, Big-Ears wasn't here. It was you who solved all the problems."

Noddy beamed. Mr Sham was right. If he could
solve one problem, he could solve others! He
picked up his kite kit, determined to put it together
all by himself.

"Goodbye, Noddy," said Mr Sham, picking
up his new shelf. "Good luck with your kit."

Big-Ears chuckled as he changed back into his usual clothes.

"Lucky Noddy didn't see through my disguise as Mr Sham!" he said to himself. "He found out something very important today. I hope he doesn't forget how good it feels to do things for himself."

Noddy did feel good making his kite. When it was finished, it looked so great he couldn't wait to show it to Big-Ears.

"Hello, Noddy. I'm back. Do you need any help?" said Big-Ears.

"No thanks. Look, I've made a kite… all by myself. Want to come and fly it with me?"

"I'd like to, Noddy, but I have a new shelf to put up,"
smiled Big-Ears. "Bye now. And have fun!"
"I will, thanks," said Noddy, and drove off, singing:
The best part is I don't need help,
'cause I can do things by myself.

First published in Great Britain by HarperCollins Publishers Ltd in 2003

5 7 9 10 8 6 4

This edition published by HarperCollins Children's Books
HarperCollins Children's Books is a division of HarperCollins Publishers Ltd.

ISBN: 0 00 712241 1

A CIP catalogue for this title is available from the British Library.

Printed and bound by Printing Express Ltd., Hong Kong

make way for

Collect them all!

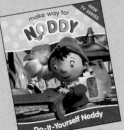

Do-It-Yourself Noddy
ISBN 0 00 712241 1

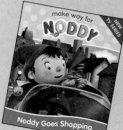

Noddy Goes Shopping
ISBN 0 00 712242 X

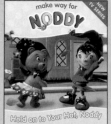

Hold on to your Hat, Noddy
ISBN 0 00 712243 8

The Magic Powder
ISBN 0 00 715101 2

Noddy and the Magic Bagpipes
ISBN 0 00 712366 3

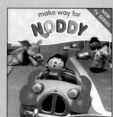

Noddy and the New Taxi
ISBN 0 00 712239 X

Bounce Alert in Toy Town
ISBN 0 00 715103 9

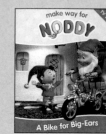

A Bike for Big-Ears
ISBN 0 00 715105 5

Noddy's Perfect Gift
ISBN 0 00 712365 5

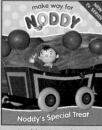

Noddy's Special Treat
ISBN 0 00 712362 0

Noddy on the Move
ISBN 0 00 715678 2

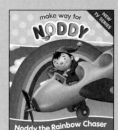

Noddy the Rainbow Chaser
ISBN 0 00 715677 4

And send off for your free Noddy poster (rrp £3.99).
Simply collect 4 tokens and complete the coupon below.

Make Way for Noddy videos now available at all good retailers